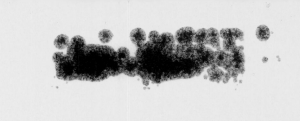

Mighty Mole

and Super Soil

By Mary Quattlebaum

Illustrated by Chad Wallace

Dawn Publications

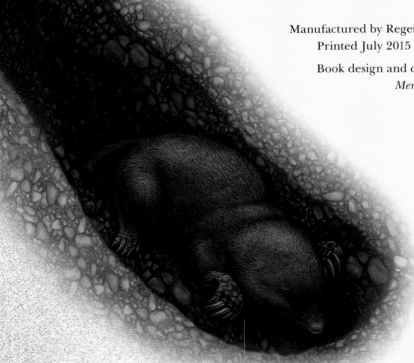

*To my brother Mel, with many thanks for
lively chats about moles — MQ*

*To my wife Ewelina, whose strength and
love is my inspiration — CW*

Copyright © 2015 Mary Quattlebaum

Illustrations copyright © 2015 Chad Wallace

Library of Congress Cataloging-in-Publication Data

Quattlebaum, Mary.

Mighty Mole and Super Soil / by Mary Quattlebaum ; illustrated by Chad Wallace. -- First edition.

pages cm

Summary: "Although considered by some to be pests, moles are highly beneficial animals, very strong and remarkable in many ways. This picture book presents the fictional, yet scientifically accurate story of a mole. Back material presents educational activities for children and background information for parents and teachers"-- Provided by publisher.

Includes bibliographical references.

ISBN 978-1-58469-538-7 (hardback) -- ISBN 978-1-58469-539-4 (pbk.) 1. Moles (Animals)--Juvenile fiction. [1. Moles (Animals)--Fiction.] I. Wallace, Chad, illustrator. II. Title.

PZ10.3.Q36Mi 2015

[E]--dc23

2014048927

Manufactured by Regent Publishing Services, Hong Kong, Printed July 2015 in ShenZhen, Guangdong, China

Book design and computer production by Patty Arnold, *Menagerie Design & Publishing*

10 9 8 7 6 5 4 3 2 1
First Edition

DAWN PUBLICATIONS
12402 Bitney Springs Road
Nevada City, CA 95959
530-274-7775
nature@dawnpub.com

Mighty Mole
and Super Soil

Below your feet,
    below stones and grass and roots,
    down
        in the moist, black ground
        Mighty Mole is on the move.

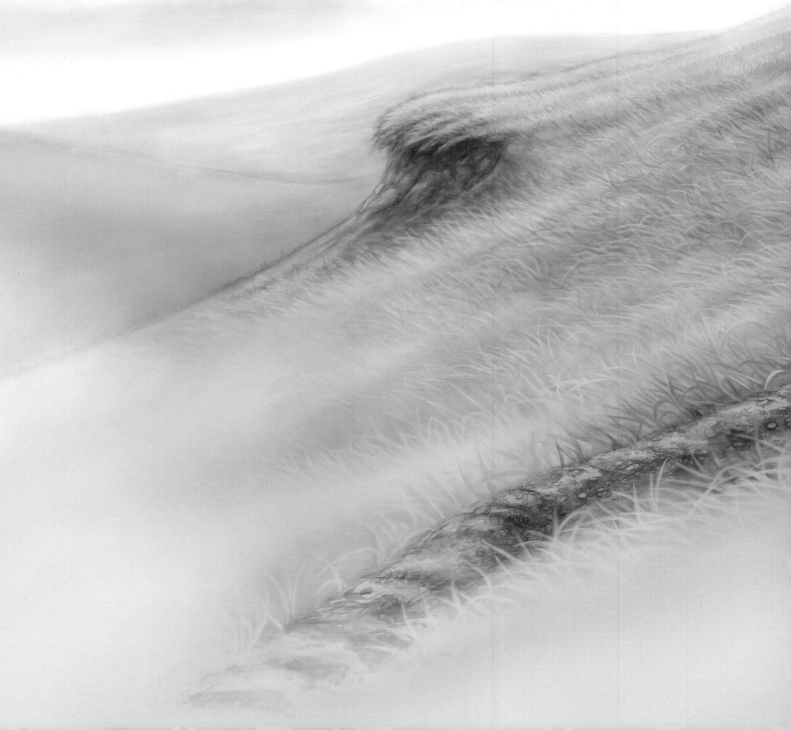

Moles dig two types of tunnels: surface and deep. Moles use surface tunnels, which are only 1 to 4 inches deep, when searching for food. As they remove or push out the soil, they create molehills.

With feet like flippers
and long, sharp claws,
Mighty Mole scratches the soil
and pushes it aside.
Scratch.
Push.
Scratch.
Push.

It is very dark,
but Mighty Mole
does not need to see.

Sniff. Sniff.
She smells something
wiggling nearby.

Moles can move things that are 35 times heavier than they are. Almost blind, they see only light and dark. Strong senses of smell and touch help them find food and avoid predators. They feel their way with sensitive whiskers and small snout bumps. Their tails sense vibrations.

Food!
Mighty Mole speeds up.
Scratch, push.
Scratch, push.
Her strong snout
digs into the soil.

The soil slides off
her soft, sleek fur.
Faster, faster!

Moles dig fast—up to 18 feet an
hour with the help of an extra thumb.
They run fast through their tunnels too—up
to 80 feet in a minute. They run backwards almost
as quickly as forwards. Their velvety fur is short and thick,
so dirt doesn't stick and slow them down.

Peck-peck-peck.
Mighty Mole feels the earth tremble.
Another creature wants her food!

Snatch!
Mighty Mole seizes
one end
of the earthworm.
A beak thrusts down and
grabs the other.
Tug!
Pull!
Mighty Mole hangs on
with her strong teeth . . .

Moles are *insectivores*. This means they eat insects, snails, slugs, centipedes, and *larvae*, also known as grubs. Moles' toxic saliva paralyzes their prey. Their favorite food is the soft, plentiful earthworm.

. . . and the bird
finally lets go.
Mighty Mole gobbles
up the juicy worm.

Moles and earthworms
help mix and *aerate*, or bring air
into, the soil when they tunnel. This helps
water to flow more easily and plants to grow.

A meadow mouse scurries along
Mighty Mole's surface tunnel,
looking for grass roots
to nibble.

A box turtle climbs out
of her hibernation hole
nearby.

Now, it's time for Mighty Mole to dig again —
not another shallow tunnel,
   but a new tunnel,
   a deep
     tunnel.

Down,
   down,
      down.

Sometimes moles get blamed for eating plant roots and flower bulbs. But it is really meadow mice that eat plants. Moles dig deep tunnels to make nests and for protection from cold and heat.

A ground beetle
digs, too,

and a wolf spider
rests in his hole.

Mighty Mole
passes an ant colony.

All this digging
makes her hungry!
She stops to eat a slow, soft grub.

Meanwhile,
down below,
a woodchuck

grooms her
kits.

Moles weigh about 5 ounces and often eat their weight in food every day. They will die unless they eat every few hours. Moles are very active for four hours, then rest for about four hours, throughout the day and night.

What's that?
A hungry snake
is squeezing
through the tunnel!
His forked tongue
flicks,
helping him to smell.
Will he find
Mighty Mole?

Mighty Mole runs
and slips
into a side tunnel.
Safe!

Snakes often hunt in tunnels in search of meadow mice, woodchuck kits, and moles. Moles are so fast that snakes rarely catch them.

Mighty Mole rests,
then begins to dig again.
She strokes through the soil
like a swimmer.
Scratch, push.
Scratch, push.

She lifts and mixes
rock chips,
pieces of plants,
bits of dead animals,
and poop.

The soil
is her home,
and Mighty Mole
helps to make it healthy.

Deep tunnels are 5 to 12 inches deep—very deep for a mole that is only 7 inches long. That's like you digging a tunnel—with your hands and feet—that's twice as tall as you are! A mole's digging helps to spread nutrients for plants.

Around Mighty Mole
are billions
of creatures
too small to see.

They break down
dead stuff—sticks,
old leaves,
and parts of animals.

Like Mighty Mole,
they enrich the soil.

Soil is alive! If you pick up a handful of healthy soil, it holds more tiny creatures than all the people on Earth. Most are so tiny you need a microscope to see them, as shown above.

Below your feet,
  below stones and grass and roots,
    down,
        down,
            down,
            in a leaf-lined nest,
            Mighty Mole
              gives birth
                to four naked pups.

Moles, like all mammals, need
to breathe air. Yet there is not much
air down there. Do they suffocate? No, because
their blood is specially adapted for breathing underground.

The pups drink her milk.
They will grow
and grow and GROW
until they are

Mighty Moles

ready to scratch,
    dig, tunnel, eat,
    and help create
healthy soil
    just like their Mighty Mom.

The Underground Community

There's a whole world beneath your feet! Every member of the underground community or *ecosystem* is important—plants, worms, insects, spiders, reptiles, mammals, and creatures too small to see.

Match each set of three clues with one of the underground critters.

Answers at www.dawnpub.com and click on "Activities"

EARTHWORM

EASTERN MOLE

SOIL MICROBES

ANT

WOLF SPIDER

GARTER SNAKE

GROUND BEETLE

MEADOW MOUSE

BOX TURTLE

WOODCHUCK

I'm a reptile that can grow up to four feet long.
Some of my favorite foods are mice and bird eggs.
I swallow my prey whole.

I breathe through my wet skin. But if the ground gets too wet, I might drown.
When I wiggle through the soil, I keep the soil loose and rich.
Moles like to eat me. So do some birds, snakes, and box turtles.

I have a hairy body and eight legs.
My large eyes can see in four directions at one time.
Some birds, snakes, and lizards like to eat me.

I spend almost all of my time underground.
My tunnels help the soil by mixing and loosening it.
I eat grubs and insects that damage plants. My favorite food is earthworms.

I'm a reptile that lives as long as 100 years.
My shell is soft when I'm young and gets harder as I get older.
When I'm young, I'm eaten by some birds and snakes.

I sometimes use mole tunnels to travel underground.
Moles get blamed for the damage I do to lawns and gardens.
I'm food for birds, snakes, and foxes.

I'm an insect and lay my eggs underground.
I'm a good digger and a fast runner.
My mouthparts are adapted for eating insects, worms, and snails.

There are lots of us in the soil.
Some of us are so tiny that we're only as big as one cell.
We eat dead plants and animals.

I live in a colony. Each member has a special job to do.
The queen's job is to lay eggs.
Workers build tunnels using their mouthparts.

I'm a large rodent also called a groundhog.
I make deeper tunnels and burrows than moles do.
My tunnel system has many exits so I can escape from predators.

Mighty Mole

Human superheroes in comic books may be able to lift cars, use X-ray vision, and leap tall buildings. Moles have super powers, too — amazing traits that help them survive. Discover what they are by closely reading each page in the story.

Super Digger: What two types of tunnels do moles make? How do moles use their snouts and paws to make tunnels? What motion do they make?

Super Strength: How much weight can a mole move? (That's like you moving an elephant!)

Super Senses: Moles rely on what two senses to help them find food and avoid predators? How do their whiskers, snout, and tail help?

Super Speed: How fast can moles dig? How fast can they move? Can they run fast backwards as well as forwards? Why is speed important?

Super Fur: How does their fur help moles to move quickly underground?

Super Eater: How much do moles eat a day? What is their favorite food?

Super Active: How often do moles sleep and for how long?

Super Saliva: How does a mole's saliva help it get food?

If you could have one of Mighty Mole's super traits, which would you want? Why?

Super Soil

Soil is found all over the world! It's like the skin of the earth. The hot Sahara Desert has soil. So does the cold Arctic tundra. Mountains and prairies also have soil. There is soil in country fields and city parks. Most of Earth's creatures, especially tiny ones, live in the soil.

Underground creatures create healthy soil for plants. Their digging and tunnel-making mixes nutrients in the soil. Digging also makes the soil loose and lets in air. This makes it easier for roots to push through the soil and for water to flow to the plants. The creatures' poop and dead bodies help make the soil more fertile.

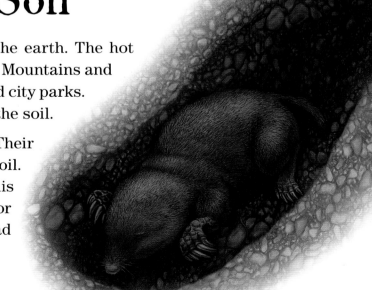

More About Super Soil

Is Soil Dirt? Soil scientists say that dirt is soil that is out of place, similar to the definition of a weed as a plant out of place (even a rose in a cornfield is a weed).

How Do Soils Form? CLORPT! This stands for *Climate*, *Organisms*, *Relief*, *Parent material*, and *Time*, which are the factors that cause soils to be different.

- *Climate* is mostly about how hot or cold and wet or dry the area is.

- *Organisms* include trees and grasses, and animals that live in the soil such as Mighty Mole, earthworms, and microbes.

- *Relief* means whether the soil is forming on the top or side of a hill, or on level ground.

- Some *parent materials* are transported tens, hundreds, or thousands of miles before they are deposited as sediments by wind, water and glaciers, while other parent materials weather in place (change into other minerals and/or break into smaller pieces) from rocks and minerals.

- It can take lots of *time* — hundreds or thousands of years for all these factors to form a soil on the land surface.

Why Soil Is Important: Soil has nutrients that are necessary for the growth of plants such as grass, flowers, trees, ferns, corn, tomatoes, wheat, and berry bushes. It also holds these plants in place. Plants provide food and oxygen for people and animals. Plants such as cotton and flax provide fiber for our clothes. Trees provide wood for houses and furniture and wood pulp for paper and books. Without soil, everyone would be hungry, naked, and homeless. (See Dr. Dirt's youtube channel. youtube.com/drdirtsoilvideos.)

How Big Are Soil Particles? All soils have a texture — a specific combination of sand, silt, and clay. Sand particles are large and feel gritty. Sand helps air and water move in soil. Silt particles are small, and feel smooth like flour or baby powder. Silt helps soil hold water for plants. Clay particles are very, very small, and hold to one another very tightly. When wet, clays are sticky and moldable like modeling clay. Clay helps soil hold nutrients and water for plants. With practice, you can learn to feel the texture of a soil caused by the differences in the amount of sand, silt, and clay.

Protect Soil: Soil can be damaged by construction, pollution, contaminated water, and by planting crops too frequently, which could deplete nutrients from the soil unless fertilizer or compost are added. Removing trees or grass can cause *erosion* or the wearing away of soil. Such damage affects the plants that grow there and the animals that eat the plants and live in the ground.

Visual, Language Arts, and STEM Activities

Visual and Language Arts

In the illustrations, can you find the ten creatures that are part of the underground community?

Research a creature in this book. How does it dig and what does its home look like? How does it avoid predators? Draw a picture and write a story about your animal.

Science

Stroke a dog or cat or a piece of fur both ways. Is one way smooth and easy to move your hand over and the other rough and more difficult to stroke? Stroke a piece of velvet both ways. A mole's fur is short and thick like velvet. How might this help it to move quickly through soil?

Gather twelve bean seeds, two small containers, soil (some play sand and some soil from a yard or garden) , and a paper towel. Plant four seeds in the play sand, four in the soil, and four between sheets of a moist paper towel. Put them all on the same window ledge in a random pattern, giving them the same amount of sunlight. Water every few days, when the soil in the container feels dry to your touch below the surface. Which sprouts first and grows more quickly? After a while, what happens to the bean on the paper towel? Why is soil important?

Visit an outdoor spot at different times of the year. How does the ground feel beneath your feet? Dig into the soil and gently touch it. How does it feel in winter, after a rain, or in the summer? What is its color? What plants are growing and are there insects, birds, or other creatures close by? Write, draw, or photograph what you observe and touch.

Gather a small pile of dead leaves outdoors. Visit every week. What changes do you see, feel, and smell? During two to eight months, tiny one-celled creatures will break down the leaves into smaller bits that enrich the soil.

Technology and Engineering

Moles dig like someone swimming. Try two ways of digging a surface (sideways) tunnel. First, hold the spoon with its bowl pointed up and dig sideways. Next hold the spoon like a paddle and scrape and scoop sideways or "swim" through the soil with it. Which movement allows you to dig easier and faster?

Try digging a deep tunnel with three different types of tools: a plastic shovel with a straight edge, a metal spoon, and a metal fork. Which tool allowed you to dig faster, with less effort? Which is most like a mole's paddle-like paws, with their sharp claws?

Engineering

Moles are shaped like cylinders, which have tapered ends, wider middles, and very few parts that stick out. This shape helps them to move quickly and smoothly through soil. Look at photos of seals, sea lions, and penguins. Do they have a cylinder shape, too? Does this help them move quickly through water? What about land?

Math

Moles eat their weight in food each day. A mole often weighs about 5 ounces, the same as a small hamster. An earthworm weighs about one-third of an ounce. If all a mole ate were earthworms, how many worms would it eat a day? [5 oz ÷ 1/3 oz /earthworm = 15 earthworms] How many a year? [15 worms/day x 365 days = 5,475/yr.] How much do you weigh? How much does your favorite food weigh? If you were to eat your own weight in food every day, calculate to see how much of this food you would need to eat. How much would you eat in one year?

Moles sleep for four hours and then they're awake for four hours throughout the day and night. In one day (24 hours), how many hours would they sleep? [Equal time waking and sleeping = 12 hours of sleeping in one day]

Moles have one litter a year, with four pups. Meadow mice have 12 litters a year, with six pups in each. In one year, how many pups will a mole give birth to? [4 pups] How about a meadow mouse? [12 x 6 = 72 pups]

Resources

Clay Robinson, PhD, aka Dr. Dirt, is the Education Manager with the American Society of Agronomy and the Soil Science Society of America. He is passionate to share the importance of soil with thousands of children. His website, doctordirt.org, is packed with teaching resources and activities. Videos are available at youtube.com/drdirtsoilvideos.

Dig It! The Secret of Soil, http://forces.si.edu/soils/, is sponsored by the National Museum of Natural History and includes information, videos, and games.

The Soil Science Society of America offers games, experiments, and career information at www.soils4kids.org and educational materials at www.soils4teachers.org.

Educators: There are many useful resources online for most of Dawn's books, including activities and lesson plans. Scan this code to go directly to activities for this book, or go to www.dawnpub.com and click on "Activities" for this and other books.

MARY QUATTLEBAUM grew up in the country surrounded by woods and a meadow. She first learned about soil, plants, and wildlife by helping to tend her family's large vegetable garden and planting wildlife gardens as 4-H projects. Mary now lives in Washington, DC, where she and her family enjoy the birds, squirrels, butterflies, cottontail rabbits, moles, and other wild visitors to their backyard habitat. She is the author of many children's books, including the *Jo MacDonald* nature series published by Dawn Publications. She teaches in the Vermont College MFA program in Writing for Children and Young Adults. Mary loves visiting schools and talking with kids. See her website www.maryquattlebaum.com.

CHAD WALLACE grew up hiking and camping in Bear Mountain, New York, just west of the Hudson River. He loves the outdoors and frequently creates art inspired by natural settings. His art invites the viewer to experience emotions from the point of view of his subjects. Chad earned a BFA degree from Syracuse University and a master's degree at the Fashion Institute of Technology. He has illustrated nine books and is also the author of one, *The Mouse and the Meadow*. His earlier books for Dawn Publications were crafted with traditional media. In this book, as with *The Mouse and the Meadow*, he has made a full transition to electronic art by simultaneously preparing the book for print, ebook, and app/game editions.

OTHER BOOKS BY MARY QUATTLEBAUM

Jo MacDonald Saw a Pond—Old MacDonald had a . . . *pond?* Yes, and now he and his granddaughter learn about wild creatures at the farm pond. E-I-E-I-O!

Jo MacDonald Hiked in the Woods—Grandpa and granddaughter explore the woods and the farm, a favorite place to take a walk. E-I-E-I-O!

Jo MacDonald Had a Garden—Oh yes, there's a vegetable garden too, where young Jo learns to grow healthy food for both people and wild creatures. E-I-E-I-O!

OTHER BOOKS BY CHAD WALLACE

The Mouse and the Meadow—Experience the vibrant and sometimes dangerous nature of meadow life from a mouse's eye-view. *This book also has a book app.*

Pass the Energy, Please!—Everybody is somebody's lunch. This perennial favorite of teachers portrays food chains of varying lengths, but they all start with the green plant.

A FEW OTHER BOOKS FROM DAWN

Over on a Mountain—Discover twenty cool animals, ten great mountain ranges, and seven continents all in one story! This is one of seven best-selling books in Marianne Berkes' "Over" series that also includes the arctic, forests, oceans, jungles, rivers, and Australia.

Under One Rock—A fascinating community of critters lives just out of sight, under rocks. Here is a low-cost "field trip between covers," part of the "Mini-habitat" series by Tony Fredericks that looks at communities on one flower, near one cattail, around one log, in one tidepool, and around one cactus.

Noisy Bird Sing-Along—Every bird has their very own kind of sound! Learn them and join in the sing-along! This is part of John Himmelman's "Noisy Sing-Along" trilogy. The other books feature noisy frogs—they can be very loud without ever opening their mouths—and noisy bugs, that can make a racket without really "singing" at all.

Pitter and Patter—Twin drops take very different rides through a watershed and around the water cycle. Along with *A Drop Around the World*, these two water cycle books are favorites with teachers and children alike.

Dawn Publications is dedicated to inspiring in children a deeper understanding and appreciation for all life on Earth. You can browse through our titles, download resources for teachers, and order at www.dawnpub.com or call 800-545-7475.